FIC   Graves, John, 1920-
         The last running

$16.95

DATE			

21 DAY LOAN

NO REISSUE

THE LAST RUNNING

THE LAST RUNNING

A story by
John Graves

Drawings by
John Groth

Lyons & Burford, Publishers

Fic

Library of Congress
Cataloging-in-Publication Data

Graves, John, 1920–   *R00733 60186*
The last running: a story/by John Graves; drawings by John Groth.   p.   cm.
ISBN 1-55821-061-X: $16.95
I. Groth, John, 1908–   . II. Title.
[PS3557.R2867L3   1990] 813′.54—dc20
89-29479   CIP

Text design by Heidi Haeuser
Printed in the United States of America

16.95

Books by John Graves

GOODBYE TO A RIVER *(1960)*

THE WATER HUSTLERS
(1970, with Robert H. Boyle and T. H. Watkins)

THE LAST RUNNING *(1974, Encino Press edition)*

HARD SCRABBLE *(1974)*

TEXAS HEARTLAND: A Hill Country Year
(1975, with Jim Bones, photographer)

FROM A LIMESTONE LEDGE *(1980)*

BLUE AND SOME OTHER DOGS *(1981)*

OF BIRDS AND TEXAS
(1986, with Stuart and Scott Gentling, painters)

THE LAST RUNNING

They called him Pajarito, in literal trader-Spanish interpretation of his surname, or more often Tom Tejano, since he had been there in those early fighting days before the Texans had flooded up onto the plains in such numbers that it became no longer practical to hate them with specificity.

After the first interview, when he had climbed down from the bed where an aching liver held him and had gone out onto the porch to salute them, only to curse in outrage and clump back into the house when he heard what they wanted, the nine of them sat like grackles about the broad gray-painted steps and talked, in Comanche, about Tom Texan the Little Bird and the antique times before wire fences had partitioned the prairies. At least, old Juan the cook said that was what they were talking about.

Mostly it was the old men who talked, three of them, one so decrepit that he had had to make the trip from Oklahoma in a lopsided carryall drawn by a piebald mare, with an odd long bundle sticking out the back, the rest riding alongside on ponies. Of the other six, two were middle-aged and four were young.

Their clothes ran a disastrous gamut from buckskin to faded calico and blue serge, but under dirty Stetsons they wore their hair long and braided, plains style. Waiting, sucking Durham cigarettes

9

and speaking Comanche, they sat about the steps and under the cottonwoods in the yard and ignored those of us who drifted near to watch them, except the one or two whom they considered to have a right to their attention. Twice a day for two days they built fires and broiled unsymmetrical chunks of the fat calf which, from his bed, furiously, Tom Bird had ordered killed for them. At night—it was early autumn—they rolled up in blankets about the old carryall and slept on the ground.

"They show any signs of leaving?" Tom Bird asked me when I went into his room toward evening of the second day.

I said, "No, sir. They told Juan they thought you could spare one easily enough, since all of them and the land too used to be theirs."

"They didn't used to be nobody's!" he shouted.

"They've eaten half that animal since they got here," I said. "I never saw anybody that could eat meat like that, and nothing but meat."

"No, nor ever saw anything else worth seeing," he said, his somber gray eyes brooding. He was one of the real ones, and none of them are left now. That was in the twenties; he was my great-uncle, and at sixteen he had run away from his father's farm in

Mississippi to work his way to the brawling acquisitive Texas frontier. At the age of eighty-five he possessed—more or less by accident, since cattle rather than land had always meant wealth to him—a medium-large ranch in the canyon country where the Cap Rock falls away to rolling prairies, south of the Texas Panhandle. He had buried two wives and had had no children and lived there surrounded by people who worked for him. When I had showed up there, three years before the Comanches' visit, he had merely grunted at me on the porch, staring sharply at my frail physique, and had gone right on arguing with his manager about rock salt in the pastures. But a month later, maybe when he decided I was going to pick up weight and live, we had abruptly become friends. He was given to quick gruff judgments and to painful retractions.

11

He said in his room that afternoon, "God damn it. I'll see them in hell before they get one, deeper than you can drop an anvil."

"You want me to tell them that?"

"Hell, yes," he said. "No. Listen, have you talked any with that old one? Starlight, they call him."

I said that neither Starlight nor the others had even glanced at any of us.

Tom Bird said, "You tell him you're kin to me. He knows a lot, that one."

"What do you want me to say about the buffalo?"

"Nothing," he said and narrowed his eyes as a jab of pain shot through him from that rebellious organ which was speaking loudly now of long-gone years of drinking at plains mudholes and Kansas saloons. He grunted. "Not a damn thing," he said. "I already told them."

Starlight paid no attention at all when I first spoke to him. I had picked up a poor grade of Spanish from old Juan in three years but was timid about using it, and to my English he showed a weathered and not even disdainful profile.

I stated my kinship to Tom Bird and said that Tom Bird had told me to speak to him.

12

Starlight stared at the fourteen pampered bison grazing in their double-fenced pasture near the house, where my great-uncle could watch them from his chair in the evenings. He had bred them from seed stock given him in the nineties by Charles Goodnight, and the only time one of them had ever been killed and eaten was when the governor of the state and a historical society had driven out to give the old man some sort of citation. When the Comanches under Starlight had arrived, they had walked down to the pasture fence and had looked at the buffalo for perhaps two hours, hardly speaking, studying the cows and the one calf and the emasculated males and the two bulls—old Shakespeare, who had killed a horse once and had put innumerable men up mesquite trees and over fences, and his lecherous though rarely productive son, John Milton.

Then they had said, matter-of-factly, that they wanted one of the animals.

Starlight's old-man smell was mixed with something wild, perhaps wood smoke. His braids were a soiled white. One of the young men glanced at me after I had spoken and said something to him in Comanche. Turning then, the old Indian looked at me down his swollen nose. His face was hexagonal and broad, but

13

sunken where teeth were gone. He spoke.

The young man said in English with an exact accent, "He wants to know what's wrong with old Tom Bird, not to talk to friends."

All of them were watching me, the young ones with more affability than the others. I said Tom Bird was sick in the liver, and patted my own.

Starlight said in Spanish, "Is he dying?"

I answered in Spanish that I didn't think so but that it was painful.

He snorted much like Tom Bird himself and turned to look again at the buffalo in the pasture. The conversation appeared to have ended, but not knowing how to leave I sat there on the top step beside the old Comanche, the rest of them ranged below us and eyeing me with what I felt to be humor. I took out cigarettes and offered them to the young man, who accepted the package and passed it along, and when it got back to me it was nearly empty. I got the impression that this gave them amusement, too, though no one had smiled. We all sat blowing smoke into the crisp evening air.

17

Then, it seemed, some ritual biding time had passed. Old Starlight began to talk again. He gazed at the buffalo in the pasture under the fading light and spoke steadily in bad Spanish with occasional phrases of worse English. The young Indian who had translated for me in the beginning lit a small stick fire below the steps. From time to time one of the other old men would obtrude a question or a correction, and they would drop into the angry Comanche gutturals, and the young man, whose name was John Oak Tree, would tell me what they were saying.

The story went on for an hour or so; when Starlight stopped talking they trooped down to the carryall and got their blankets and rolled up in them on the ground. In the morning I let my work in the ranch office wait and sat down again with the Comanches on the steps, and Starlight talked

18

again. The talk was for me, since I was Tom Bird's kinsman. Starlight did not tell the story as I tell it here. Parts I had to fill in later in conversation with Tom Bird, or even from books. But this was the story.

Without knowing his exact age, he knew that he was younger than Tom Bird, about the age of dead Quanah Parker, under whom he had more than once fought. He had come to warrior's age during the big fight the white men had had among themselves over the black men. Born a Penateka or Honey Eater while the subtribal divisions still had meaning, he remembered the surly exodus from the Brazos reservation to Oklahoma in 1859, the expulsion by law of the Comanches from all of Texas.

But white laws had not meant much for another ten years or so. It was a time of blood and confusion, a good time to be a Comanche and fight the most lost of all causes. The whites at the Oklahoma agencies were Northern and not only tolerated but sometimes egged on and armed the parties striking down across the Red, with the full moon, at the line of settlements established

19

by the abominated and tenacious Texans. In those days, Starlight said, Comanches held Texans to be another breed of white men, and even after they were told that peace had smiled again among whites, they did not consider this to apply to that race which had swarmed over the best of their grass and timber.

In the beginning, the raids had ritual formality and purpose; an individual party would go south either to make war, or to steal horses, or to drive off cattle for trading to the New Mexican *comancheros* at plains rendezvous, or maybe just reminiscently to run deer and buffalo over the old grounds. But the distinctions dimmed. In conservative old age Starlight believed that the Comanches' ultimate destruction was rooted in the loss of the old disciplines. That and smallpox and syphilis and whiskey. And Mackenzie's soldiers. All those things ran in an apocalyptic pack, like wolves in winter.

They had gone horse raiding down into the Brazos country, a dozen of them, all young and all good riders and fighters. They captured thirty horses here and there in the perfect stealth that pride demanded, without clashes, and were headed back north up the Keechi Valley near Palo Pinto when a Texan with a yellow beard caught them in his corral at dawn and killed two of them

22

with a shotgun. They shot the Texan with arrows; Starlight himself peeled off the yellow scalp. Then, with a casualness bred of long cruelty on both sides, they killed his wife and two children in the log house. She did not scream as white women were said to do, but until a hatchet cleaved her skull kept shouting, "Git out! Git, git, git."

And collecting five more horses there, they continued the trek toward the Territory, driving at night and resting at known secret spots during the days.

The leader was a son of old Iron Shirt, Pohebits Quasho, bullet-dead on the Canadian despite his Spanish coat of mail handed down from the old haughty days. Iron Shirt's son said that it was bad to have killed the woman and the children, but Starlight, who with others laughed at him, believed even afterward that it would have been the same if they had let the woman live.

What was certain was that the Texans followed, a big party with men among them who could cut trail as cleanly as Indians. They followed quietly, riding hard and resting little, and on the third evening, when the Comanches were gathering their herd and readying themselves to leave a broad enclosed creek valley where they had spent the day, their sentry on a hill yelled and was dead,

23

and the lean horsemen with the wide hats were pouring down the hillside shouting the long shout that belonged to them.

When it happened, Starlight was riding near the upper end of the valley with the leader. The only weapons with them were their knives and Starlight's lance, with whose butt he had been poking the rumps of the restive stolen horses as they hazed them toward camp below. As they watched, the twenty or more Texans over-rode the camp, and in the shooting and confusion the two Co-manches heard the end of their five companions who had been there afoot.

"I knew this," the leader said.

"You knew it," Starlight answered him bitterly. "You should have been the sentry, Know-much."

Of the other two horse gatherers, who had been working the lower valley, they could see nothing, but a group of the Texans rode away from the camp in that direction, yelling and firing.

25

Then others broke toward Starlight and the leader a half mile above.

"We can run around them to the plain below," the son of Iron Shirt said. "Up this creek is bad."

Starlight did not know the country up the creek, but he knew what he felt, and feeling for a Comanche was conviction. He turned his pony upstream and spurred it.

"Ragh!" he called to the leader in farewell. "You're dirty luck!" And he was right, for he never saw the son of Iron Shirt again. Or the other two horse gatherers either.

But the son of Iron Shirt had been right, too, because ten minutes later Starlight was forcing his pony among big fallen boulders in a root tangle of small steep canyons, each of which carried a trickle to the stream below. There was no way even to lead a horse up their walls; he had the feeling that any one of them would bring him to a blind place.

Behind him shod hoofs rang; he whipped the pony on, but a big Texan on a bay horse swept fast around a turn in the canyon, jumping the boulders, and with a long lucky shot from a pistol broke Starlight's pony's leg. The Comanche fell with the pony but lit cat-bouncing and turned, and as the Texan came down waited crouched with the lance. The Texan had one of the pistols that shot six times, rare then in that country. Bearing down, he fired three times, missing each shot, and then when it was the moment Starlight feinted forward and watched the Texan lurch aside from the long bright blade, and while he was off balance, Starlight drove it into the Texan's belly until it came out the back. The blade snapped as the big man's weight came onto it, falling.

27

Starlight sought the pistol for a moment but not finding it ran to the canyon wall and began climbing. He was halfway up the fifty feet of its crumbling face when the other Texan rode around the turn and stopped, and from his unquiet horse, too hastily, fired a rifle shot that blew Starlight's left eye full of powdered sandstone.

He was among swallows' nests. Their molded mud crunched under his hands; the birds flew in long loops, chittering about his head. Climbing, he felt the Texan's absorbed reloading behind and below him as the horse moved closer, and when he knew with certainty that it was time, looked around to see the long caplock rifle rising again. . . . Watched still climbing, and guessing at the instant, wrenched himself hard to the right, seizing the roots of a cedar that grew almost at the top of the cliff.

28

The bullet smashed through his upper left arm, and he hung only by his right, but with the long wiry strength of trick horsemanship he swung himself up and onto the overhanging turf of the cliff's top. A round rock the size of a buffalo's head lay there. Almost without pausing he tugged it loose from the earth and rolled it back over the cliff. It came close. The Texan grabbed the saddle as his horse reared, and dropped his rifle. They looked at each other. Clutching a blood-greasy, hanging arm, the Comanche stared down at a big nose and a pair of angry gray eyes, and the young Texan stared back.

Wheeling, Starlight set off trotting across the hills. That night before hiding himself he climbed a low tree and quavered for hours like a screech owl, but no one answered. A month later, an infected skeleton, he walked into the Penateka encampment at Fort Sill, the only one of twelve to return.

That had been his first meeting with Tom Bird.

hen telling of the fights, Starlight stood up and gestured in proud physical representation of what he and others had done. He did not give it as a story with a point; it was the recountal of his acquaintance with a man. In the bug-flecked light of a bulb above the house's screen door the old Indian should have looked absurd—hipshot, ugly, in a greasy black hat and a greasy dark suit with a gold chain across its vest, the dirty braids flying as he creaked through the motions of long-unmeaningful violence.

But I did not feel like smiling. I looked at the younger Indians expecting perhaps to find amusement among them, or boredom, or cynicism. It was not there. They were listening, most of them probably not even understanding the Spanish but knowing the stories, to an ancient man who belonged to a time when their race had been literally terrible.

In the morning Starlight told of the second time. It had been after the end of the white men's war; he was a war chief with bull horns on his head. Thirty well-armed warriors rode behind him when he stopped a trail herd in the Territory for tribute. Although the cowmen were only eight, their leader, a man with a black mustache, said that four whoa-haws were too many. He would give maybe two.

31

"Four," Starlight said. "Texan."

It was an arraignment, and the white man heard it as such. Looking at the thirty Comanches, he said that he and his people were not Texans but Kansas men returning home with bought cattle.

"Four whoa-haws," Starlight said.

The white man made a sullen sign with his hand and spoke to his men, who went to cut out the steers. Starlight watched jealously to make certain they were not culls, and when three of his young men had them and were driving them away, he rode up face to face with the white leader, unfooled even though the mustache was new.

"Tejano," he said. "Stink sonabitch." And reached over and twisted Tom Bird's big nose, hard, enjoying the rage barely held in the gray eyes. He patted his scarred left biceps and saw that the white man knew him, too, and reached over to twist the nose again, Tom Bird too prudent to stop him and too proud to duck his head aside.

"Tobacco, Texan," Starlight said.

32

Close to snarling, Tom Bird took out a plug. After sampling and examining it and picking a bit of lint from its surface, Starlight tucked it into his waistband. Then he turned his horse and, followed by his thirty warriors, rode away.

In those days revenge had still existed.

He had been, too, with Quanah Parker when the half-white chief had made a separate peace with Tom Bird—Tom Tejano the Pajarito now, looming big on the high plains—as with a government, on the old Bird range up along the Canadian. There had been nearly two hundred with Quanah on a hunt in prohibited territory, and they found few buffalo and many cattle. After the peace with Tom Bird they had not eaten any more wing-branded

36

beef, except later when the Oklahoma agency bought Bird steers to distribute among them.

They had clasped hands there in Quanah's presence, knowing each other well, and in the cowman's tolerant grin and the pressure of his hard fingers Starlight had read more clearly the rout of his people than he had read it anywhere else before.

"Yah, Big-nose," he said, returning the grip and the smile. Tom Bird rode along with them hunting for ten days and led them to a wide valley twenty miles long that the hide hunters had not yet

found, and they showed him there how their fathers had run the buffalo in the long good years before the white men. November it had been, with frosted mornings and yellow bright days; their women had followed them to dress the skins and dry the meat. It was the last of the rich hunting years.

After that whenever Tom Bird passed through Oklahoma he would seek out the Indian who had once pulled his nose and would sometimes bring presents.

But Starlight had killed nine white men while the fighting had lasted.

Dressed, Tom Bird came out onto the porch at eleven o'clock, and I knew from the smooth curve of his cheek that the liver had quit hurting. He was affable and shook all their hands again.

"We'll have a big dinner at noon," he told Starlight in the same

flowing pidgin Spanish the old Comanche himself used. "Juan's making it especially for my Comanche friends, to send them on their trip full and happy."

Still unfooled, Starlight exhumed the main topic.

"No!" Tom Bird said.

"You have little courtesy," Starlight said. "You had more once."

Tom Bird said, "There were more of you then. Armed."

Starlight's eyes squinted in mirth which his mouth did not let itself reflect. Absently Tom Bird dug out his Days O' Work and bit a chew, then waved the plug apologetically and offered it to the Comanche. Starlight took it and with three remaining front teeth haggled off a chunk, and pretended to put it into his vest pocket.

They both started laughing, phlegmy, hard-earned, old men's laughter, and for the first time—never having seen Tom Bird out-argued before—I knew that it was going to work out.

Tom Bird said, "Son of a coyote, you . . . I've got four fat *castrados*, and you can have your pick. They're good meat, and I'll eat some of it with you."

Starlight waggled his head mulishly. "Those, no," he said. "The big bull."

42

Tom Bird stared, started to speak, closed his mouth, threw the returned plug of tobacco down on the porch, and clumped back into the house. The Indians all sat down again. One of the other older men reached over and picked up the plug, had a chew, and stuck it into his denim jacket. Immobility settled.

"Liberty," Starlight said out of nowhere, in Spanish. "They speak much of liberty. Not one of you has ever seen liberty, or smelled it. Liberty was grass, and wind, and a horse, and meat to hunt, and no wire."

From beyond the dark screen door Tom Bird said, "The little bull."

Starlight without looking around shook his head. Tom Bird opened the door so hard that it battered back against the house wall, loosening flakes of paint. He stopped above the old Indian and stood there on bowed legs, looking down. "You rusty old bastard!" he shouted in English. "I ain't got but the two, and the big one's the only good one. And he wouldn't eat worth a damn."

Starlight turned his head and eyed him.

"All right," Tom Bird said, slumping. "All right."

"Thank you, Pajarito," Starlight said.

"Jimmy," the old man said to me in a washed-out voice, "go

43

tell the boys to shoot Shakespeare and hang him up down by the washhouse."

"No," John Oak Tree said.

"What the hell you mean, no?" Tom Bird said, turning to him with enraged pleasure. "That's the one he wants. What you think he's been hollering about for two whole days?"

"Not dead," John Oak Tree said. "My grandfather wants him alive."

"Now ain't that sweet?" the old man said. "Ain't that just beautiful? And I can go around paying for busted fences from here to Oklahoma and maybe to the God damn Arctic Circle, all so a crazy old murdering Comanche can have him a pet bull buffalo."

Starlight spoke in Spanish, having understood most of the English. "Tom Tejano, listen," he said.

"What?"

"Listen," Starlight said. "We're going to kill him, Tom Tejano. We."

"My butt!" said Tom Bird, and sat down.

45

In the afternoon, after the fried chicken and the rice and mashed beans and the tamales and the blistering chili, after the courteous belching and the smoking on the porch, everyone on the ranch who could leave his work was standing in the yard under the cottonwoods as the nine Comanches brought their horses up from the lot, where they had been eating oats for two days, and tied them outside the picket fence, saddled.

After hitching Starlight's mare to the carryall, without paying any attention to their audience they began to strip down, methodically rolling their shed clothes into bundles with hats on top and putting them on the back of the carryall. Starlight reeled painfully among them, pointing a dried-up forefinger and giving orders. When they had finished, all of them but he wore only trousers and shoes or moccasins, with here and there scraps of the old bone and claw and hide and feather paraphernalia. John Oak Tree had slipped off the high-heeled boots he wore and replaced them with tennis sneakers.

A hundred yards away, gargling a bellow from time to time, old Shakespeare stood jammed into a chute where the hands had choused him. Between bellows, his small hating eye peered toward us from beneath a grayed board; there was not much doubt about

46

how *he* felt.

The Indians took the long, blanketed bundle from the carryall and unrolled it.

"For God's sake!" a cowboy said beside me, a man named Abe Reynolds who had worked a good bit with the little buffalo herd. "For God's sake, this is nineteen damn twenty-three?"

I chuckled. Old Tom Bird turned his gray eyes on us and glared, and we shut up. The bundle held short bows, and quivers of arrows, and long, feather-hung, newly reshafted buffalo lances daubed with red and black. Some took bows and others lances, and among the bowmen were the two old men younger than Starlight, who under dry skins still had ridged segmented muscles.

"Those?" I said in protest, forgetting Tom Bird. "Those two couldn't . . ."

"Because they never killed one," he said without looking around. "Because old as they are, they ain't old enough to have hunted the animal that for two whole centuries was the main thing their people ate, and wore, and made tents and ropes and saddles and every other damn thing they had out of. You close your mouth, boy, and watch."

Starlight made John Oak Tree put on a ribboned medal of some kind. Then they sat the restless ponies in a shifting line, motley still but somehow, now, with the feel of that old terribleness coming off of them like a smell, and Starlight walked down the line of them and found them good and turned to raise his hand at Tom Bird.

Tom Bird yelled.

The man at the chute pulled the bars and jumped for the fence, and eight mounted Indians lashed their ponies into a hard run toward the lumpy blackness that had emerged and was standing there swaying its head, bawling-furious.

Starlight screeched. But they were out of his control now and swept in too eagerly, not giving Shakespeare time to decide to run. When the Indian on the fastest pony, one of the middle-aged men, came down on him shooting what looked like a steady jet of arrows from beside the pony's neck, the bull squared at him. The Indian reined aside, but not enough. The big head came up under the pony's belly, and for a moment horse and rider paused reared against the horns and went pin-wheeling backward into the middle of the on-rushing others.

"Them idiots!" Abe Reynolds said. "Them plumb idiots!"

49

One swarming pile then, one mass with sharp projecting heads and limbs and weapons, all of them yelling and pounding and hacking and stabbing, and when old Shakespeare shot out from under the pile, shrugging them helter-skelter aside, he made a run for the house. Behind him they came yipping, leaving a gut-ripped dead horse on the ground beside the chute and another running riderless toward the northeast. One of the downed hunters sat on the ground against the chute as though indifferently. The other—one of the two oldsters—was hopping about on his left leg with an arrow through the calf of his right.

But I was scrambling for the high porch with the spectators, those who weren't grabbing for limbs, though Tom Bird stood his ground cursing as Shakespeare smashed through the white picket fence like dry sunflower stalks and whirled to make another stand under the cottonwoods. Some of the Indians jumped the fence and others poured through the hole he had made, all howling until it seemed there could be no breath left in them. For a moment, planted, Shakespeare stood with arrows bristling brightly from his hump and his loins and took someone's lance in his shoulder. Then he gave up that stand, too, and whisked out another eight feet of fence as he leveled into a long run down the dirt road past the corrals.

They rode him close, poking and shooting.

And finally, when it was all far enough down the road to have the perspective of a picture, John Oak Tree swung out leftward and running parallel to the others pulled ahead and abruptly slanted in with the long bubbling shriek, loud and cutting above all the other noise, that you can call rebel yell or cowboy holler or whatever you want, but which deadly exultant men on horseback have likely shrieked since the Assyrians and long, long before. Shakespeare ran desperately free from the sharp-pointed furor behind him, and John Oak Tree took his dun pony in a line converging sharply with the bull's course, and was there, and jammed the lance's blade certainly just behind the ribs and pointing forward, and the bull skidded to his knees, coughed, and rolled onto

52

his side.

"You call that fair?" Abe Reynolds said sourly.

Nobody had. It was not fair. Fair did not seem to have much to do with what it was.

Starlight's carryall was headed for the clump of horsemen down the road, but the rest of us were held to the yard by the erect stability of Tom Bird's back as he stood in one of the gaps in his picket fence. Beside the chute, Starlight picked up the two thrown Indians and the saddle from the dead horse, the old hunter disarrowed and bleeding now, and drove on to where the rest sat on their ponies around Shakespeare's carcass.

Getting down, he spoke to John Oak Tree. The young Indian dismounted and handed his lance to Starlight, who hopped around for a time with one foot in the stirrup and got up onto the dun pony and brought it back toward the house at a run, the lance held high. Against his greasy vest the big gold watch chain bounced, and his coattails flew, but his old legs were locked snugly around the pony's barrel. He ran it straight at Tom Bird where he stood in the fence gap, and pulled it cruelly onto its hocks three yards away, and held out the lance butt first.

"I carried it when I pulled your nose," he said. "The iron, any-

55

how."

Tom Bird took it.

"We were there, Tom Tejano," Starlight said.

"Yes," my great-uncle said. "Yes, we were there."

The old Comanche turned the pony and ran it back to the little group of his people and gave it to John Oak Tree, who helped him get back into the carryall. Someone had caught the loose pony. For a few moments all of them sat, frozen, looking down at the arrow-quilled black bulk that had been Shakespeare.

Then, leaving it there, they rode off down the road toward Oklahoma, past the fences of barbed steel that would flank them all the way.

A cowhand, surveying the deadly debris along the route of their run, said dryly, "A neat bunch of scutters, be damn if they ain't."

I was standing beside old Tom Bird, and he was crying. He felt my eyes and turned, the bloody lance upright in his hand, paying no heed to the tears running down the sides of his big nose and into his mustache.

"Damn you, boy," he said. "Damn you for not ever getting to know anything worth knowing. Damn me, too. We had a world, once."